NOW YOU CAN READ....

The Frog Prince

STORY ADAPTED BY LUCY KINCAID
ILLUSTRATED BY PAMELA STOREY

BRIMAX BOOKS • CAMBRIDGE • ENGLAND

A Princess was playing with her golden ball. She dropped it. It rolled across the grass towards the pond. She ran after it.

Before she could reach it, it fell into the pond with a gentle plop.

The Princess knelt beside the pond. She looked down into the clear water. Her golden ball was lying at the bottom of the pond like a golden sun. She tried to get it out. The pond was too deep. She could not reach it. The Princess began to cry.

"Why are you crying?" asked a voice. The Princess looked around. There was a frog sitting on a rock beside the pond.

"Did you speak?" she asked.

"I did," said the frog.

The Princess told him what had happened to her ball.

"I will fetch your ball for you
if you promise me three things,"
said the frog. "You must let me
sit on your chair. You must share
your food with me. You must let
me lie on your bed."
"Of course I will, I promise,"
said the Princess. "Now, please,
will you get my ball?"

The frog dived to the bottom of the pond.

He brought the golden ball back to the Princess. It was not easy for him. The ball was as big as he was.

The Princess took the ball from the frog. She danced off across the garden. She had already forgotten her promise. She did not give the frog another thought.

Next morning, everyone in the palace was getting ready for breakfast. The Princess was skipping along the corridor when she met the frog. "What are YOU doing in the palace?" she cried.

"You must now keep your promise," said the frog.

“Go back to the garden where you belong,” cried the Princess. “I do not like you!”

She ran and hid behind the King. “Please make the frog go away,” she said.

But when the King heard that the Princess had made a promise, he said, “A promise is a promise, and it must be kept. A promise to a frog is just as important as a promise to a king.”

The King and his three daughters sat down to eat breakfast.
The frog hopped to the side of the Princess's chair.
"May I sit beside you?" he croaked.
The King heard the frog speak and he looked sternly at the Princess.

The Princess picked
up the frog.
"Do not drop me,"
he said.
"Do not drop him,"
said the King.

The Princess put
the frog on the
chair beside her,
then moved as far
away from him as
she could.

"May I share your food?" asked the frog. The Princess put the frog on the table beside her own plate.

The frog ate a very good breakfast. The Princess ate hardly anything at all. Somehow, she did not feel very hungry.

When he had finished eating, the frog said, "I am tired. May I lie on your bed?"
The Princess did not answer. The King looked at her sternly.
"A promise is a promise," he said.

The Princess picked up the frog. She held him away from her and carried him to her bedroom.

The Princess could not bear to think of the frog sitting on her bed. She put him on a little chair away from her bed. She closed the bedroom door so that nobody could see what she had done.

"I will tell the King you have not kept your promise," croaked the frog. The Princess burst into tears. She could not help it. "I have let you sit on my chair, I have shared my food with you," she cried, "must I really let you lie on my bed?"

“A promise is a promise, as you very well know,” croaked the frog. The Princess lifted the frog from the chair and threw him across the room.

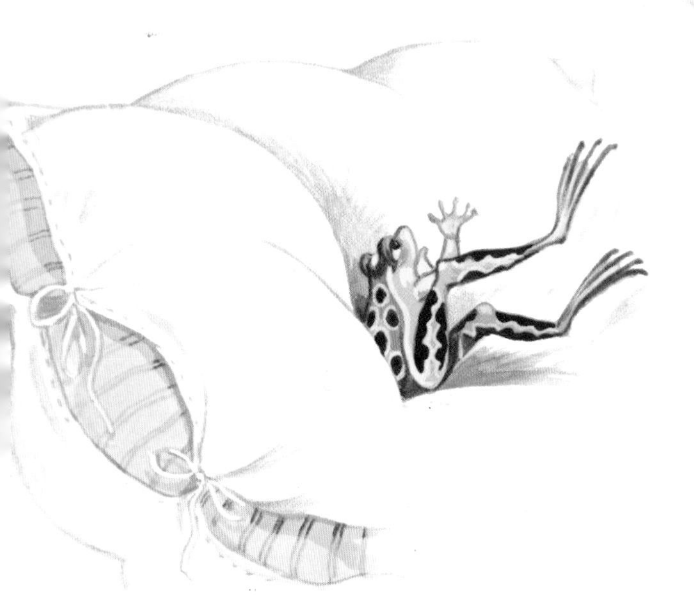

He fell onto her crisp white pillow. The Princess buried her face in her hands and cried.

She did not see the frog change into a Prince.

The Prince wiped away her tears. "By keeping your promise you have broken a spell cast by a wicked witch," he said. "Now we can both live happily ever after." And they did.

All these appear in the pages of the story. Can you find them?